Bakelite,

a Rotary Dial,

and a Party Line

♦♦♦

D. M. Weaver

This book has been changed—its title and ISBNs and can now be found here:

House on the Edge of Forever –
ISBN-13: 978-1508785262,
ISBN-10: 1508785260

Or the following links:
Paperback – Createspace:
https://www.createspace.com/5360287
Kindle – http://www.amazon.com/dp/B00UEXVO3U

Upcoming books by D. M. Weaver

Winter's Light

Anthologies #1

Anthologies #2

The Christmas Gift

Bakelite,
a Rotary Dial,
and a Party Line

◆◆◆

D. M. Weaver

http://weaverdm.weebly.com

Bookcover created E. C. Weaver

For more information on Author D. M. Weaver, visit his website at: http://weaverdm.weebly.com.

First Edition

ISBN-13: 978-1505577990
ISBN-10: 1505577993

Dedication

To families, past and present

♦♦♦

Table of Contents

Chapter 1

THE WIPERS SWUNG FROM SIDE to side in a slow arc across the windshield. No sooner had they finished when they began to swing back in the same fashion wiping away the new drops of water that were rapidly impacting the glass. Faster and harder the rain fell. Those drops missed by the wipers combined together into larger drops, racing down, dragged by gravity's incessant pull to the bottom. The clicking of the blades against the stops as they reached the ends of each arc along with the whirring of the electric motor that drove them was somehow comforting.

Dan Long sat quietly watching the small house for some time. He had been trying to decide if he really wanted to do it. Now that he was here, he wasn't sure it was worth the time.

The little house had been ravaged by the passage of time as well as by an endless procession of temporary tenets that could have cared less about the little building's upkeep. The horizontal clapboard siding that had withstood so many bitter cold winters had been replaced by that of an unknown composition and arranged so that it ran vertically up and down. This gave it the appearance of a tall, but very narrow, almost cartoonish, structure.

The chimney perched high on the four-sided, steeply pitched roof, had lost several bricks and threatened to tumble at the slightest hint of a breeze pushing against it. Many years before, great patches of the green-black asphalt shingles covering its precipitous slopes had blown away in one or another of the gales that happened through the Snake River Valley.

Gone were the four huge poplar trees that marked the edge of the property and stood as sentinels alongside the road. Their very presence proclaimed to the world, "Within are those things most precious. Ye are welcome, but only if ye be a friend."

The sidewalk that once ran from the center of the trees, where the mailbox had been mounted, to the house had long cracked and crumbled, leaving only a gray trace of gravel to indicate that it had ever existed.

Gone was Mr. Hulbert's store. It had stood next to the long gravel driveway that stretched from the main road to the eastside of the house and eventually terminated around the back.

Even the gravel of the driveway had long been worn thin revealing the brown dirt beneath. In the driving rain, it churned and blended with the water into a dark, sticky brown mud. Tire ruts that had eroded the earth by generations of vehicles' passage were now disturbed only by the rain as it slammed into the ground. Like dancers on a dance floor, their forms came together as one drop racing to the bottom, coalescing with another, and then being swallowed up in the crowd until, at the bottom, they collected into newly formed puddles.

Dan sat quietly in the car staring at the old house as the rain drummed out its song on the roof. *Why*, he thought? He let out a slow, heavy sigh, his cheeks puffing out as the air flowed out through his tight lips.

A day earlier, at the local service station, he had learned from an old family friend that the old house was due to be demolished to make way for a new housing development.

Now as he contemplated the finality of the demolition, a feeling of melancholy swept over him. After all, he had many fond memories of the old place and the wonderful people that had given it life. Even with the passage of time, many of the old memories seemed fresh and tugged at his heart.

He had not forgotten.

He was determined to get one last look at the old house before its mortal existence was brought unceremoniously to an end.

On a drive by earlier in the day, he had seen a sign that had given him the name and phone number of the developer that had bought the property. At the first opportunity, Dan had phoned the contractor. He had explained his connection to the old place and had been able to gain permission to go onto the property. So now, here he sat across the street in the elementary school parking lot, pondering what value he could derive from the excursion.

After some time of weighing the pros and cons, Dan slipped the car into drive and crossed the road into the now water-covered driveway. The faint familiar sound of the remaining gravel crunched under the car's tires.

As he pulled around to the back of the house, the old coal shed and little out-building at the back of the property came into view.

The late September sun was almost set as the dark rain-filled clouds choked out what little sunlight struggled to push its way through. The low light lent a gray, almost ghostly hue to the scene. As the car came to a stop, its headlights shone on the house's now dilapidated siding, accentuating its run down condition.

The back door to the porch stood closed, the paint peeling, the window boarded up. In the headlights he could see that the door knob had long since been pulled out leaving a dark hole. Out through the hole, a light chain hung, its end tied with some kind of wire to another section that was nailed to the door jam on the outside in a futile attempt to secure it from would be intruders.

As the car came to a rest, Dan threw it into park and shut off the engine. He sat for what seemed like an eternity taking in the whole scene. He choked back deep feelings that threatened to well up and swallow his machismo. Switching off the lights, he sat in the dark listening to the rain's light patter on the car's metal skin. His wife always accused him of having a soft heart. Perhaps it was always that way or maybe it was because of the events he had witnessed.

As a young man, fresh out of high school, Dan had served a two year mission in the South Pacific for his church. There he had seen both great successes working with the humble island peoples, as well as crushing heart breaks as many turned away from the message he shared.

On returning home, he had enrolled in college and enlisted in the R.O.T.C. program sponsored by the Army as a way to assuage the cost of his education. Upon graduation in 1989, he received his commission and was stationed at Fort Ord in California.

When he was a wet-behind-the-ears second lieutenant, he was assigned to one of the many basic training companies housed on the base. It wasn't long until his eyes were opened as to how the rest of the world operated.

In 1991, he found himself in the deserts of Kuwait as a part of Operation Desert Storm. After the campaign was over, he returned stateside to finish out his time.

In 1993, his hitch in the Army was up, and he elected to go back to school for his Master's Degree. It was there that he met Tammy, his wife. After a short courtship, they were married, and soon the children came. However, it wasn't without trial. The first three children, a boy and two girls, had come without any problems, and life seemed to be moving blissfully forward. Then their faith was tested.

Their fourth child, a little boy, was stillborn. Tammy was devastated, and there was little Dan could do to console her for a time. If it hadn't been for their shared and deep religious beliefs, they would have never been able to overcome the grief enough to move on.

Working two jobs to pay his way through school, and with the mounting medical bills, Dan reenlisted in the military to better make ends meet. This time he enlisted in the local guard unit in their community. It would take another three years for him to get his Master's Degree in Engineering. All the while, he juggled a part-time night job and his obligations to the military.

The time finally came when Dan finished his schooling and went to work for a local engineering firm. Still, he remained active in the guard. Life seemed to have mended and was moving forward when the Twin Towers fell on September 11, 2001. It wasn't long before Dan found himself again in the Middle East as a newly commissioned captain in charge of the artillery battery.

After a twelve month tour, Dan's unit was sent home, and he tried to resume his life. However, life was interrupted once more as his unit was redeployed to Afghanistan. This was his last deployment.

On return to the states, he was informed that due to his age, he could either except a promotion to Major and work stateside, overseeing the training of the members of his state's guard units, or resign his commission and return to civilian life. After considering the matter, Dan decided to except the promotion and remain in long enough to get his military retirement.

As he sat looking at the house, he mulled over the last few weeks he had spent at Fort Sill in Oklahoma. He had attended classes consisting of the latest instruction for the rapid deployment and use of artillery in U.S. Army. It had been good duty, and he had learned a lot.

He wanted to get home as soon as he could and share what he had acquired with the troops. But more importantly, he couldn't wait to get home to the family. In that respect, it had been a long time. His trip home brought him by the old town and, at Tammy's urging, he had decided to swing through town to visit his elderly aunt. Now in her early 80's, his aunt was one of two of his father's family still living.

On the second day of a three day visit, Dan had found out about the impending destruction. Now he sat in the driveway of the old house. The light of the day had faded into twilight, and the rain had died down to a mere misting on the glass. The house stood dark and foreboding.

As a young boy, Dan could remember waking up to the sound of the gravel crunching under the tires of the family station wagon as it rolled down the driveway to where he was now parked. More often than not, it was just after dark, and a soft glow would emanate from the windows of his grandparents' house. This same backdoor would be lit up by the porch light. And a half a million insects would be bouncing and swooping about it.

You see, Dan's father was a career military man, and except for the times that his dad was deployed overseas during the Vietnam War, the family spent most of their lives travelling from post to post or wherever the Army would send them. A major portion of their time was spent crammed together as a family of seven in the white American Motors station wagon. They saw a lot of the country rolling down the highways and byways of the United States.

However, the best times were when his dad got leave, and the whole family packed up and headed for grandpa and grandma's house in Idaho. The popping gravel under the tires meant home, security, but most of all, family.

With these thoughts on his mind, Dan opened the door and stepped out into the fresh, moist air scrubbed clean by the rain.

Looking around the darkened yard, he walked back to the trunk of his car and popped the lid open. The trunk light lit up the interior with a utilitarian glow. Amongst the normal accoutrements in the trunk were Dan's duffel bag and military equipment. Reaching in, he pulled his flashlight from where it was secured on his web gear.

The chill of the evening cut through the light jacket he had been wearing in the car. He quickly grabbed his field jacket and tossed the light coat into the trunk.

He donned a small, black knit cap and pulled it down around his ears. The cap was a special gift he had received from a good friend in Special Ops during one of his tours in the deserts of Iraq. He always kept it with him as a remembrance of his friend who hadn't come home.

Reaching into the pocket of the light jacket he had just discarded, he pulled out and put on the black leather driving gloves his kids had given him two Christmases before. He looked all the part of a skulking thief more than the venturing explorer he was soon to become. *Indiana Jones, look out*, he thought.

As he started to close the trunk, he remembered the Big Hunk candy bar he had bought at the convenience store a few hour before. *Poggy Bait*, he thought to himself. The words, he remembered with a laugh, always brought back visions of Sergeant Major Stephenson.

Sergeant Major Stanley Stephenson was a 'Viet Nam' retread from Tuscaloosa, Alabama. Dan had met him during his first tour of Iraq. Stephenson had been famous for branding the care packages his family had sent to him as 'Poggy Bait,' a military slang term for candy and other foods not approved for consumption by military personnel. It had a more nefarious meaning, as most military slang does, but Dan chose not to think in those terms. He preferred the watered down definition. He made it a point to never ask Stephenson how he meant it either.

When the Sergeant Major received a package of candy from home, he would shake it at Dan, and with a chuckle and a gleam in his eye, spit out the words, "Poggy Bait."

The packages were from his youngest grandsons, 10 and 12 years old. They had saved their old Halloween candy that they didn't like or some that had not been handed out during the season. Then they wrapped it in fancy paper and sent it to him as a present.

Some of it had gotten quite hard before it got to him. He had complained that he would have to make an appointment with the oral surgeon to fix his broken teeth after his tour of duty was over. When Dan pointed out that he was not bound by any special protocol to eat the candy, Stephens had mumbled something colorful under his breath and then flashed him a big grin.

Even though he put up a good front, the Sergeant Major could be counted on to be at the front of the line to get any letter or package his family would send. His wallet didn't contain a lot of money, but it did contain a grundle of pictures showing his entire posterity. And he wasn't shy about showing them off to the staff.

Stephenson had been in country longer and was cycled home a couple of months before Dan. And though they would never meet again, Dan would always value their working together. It was a good memory he would endeavor to keep fresh, while fighting to reconcile others.

Now with the candy bar retrieved and the proper equipment assembled, he was ready to begin the adventure.

Chapter 2

THE CHAIN TURNED OUT TO be nothing more than a section of old rusty dog chain looped through the hole in the door with a twisted piece of hanger tying it to the section nailed to the jam.

The whole assembly fell apart readily into his hand with little to no effort at all. *Not exactly Fort Knox*, he mused. With a slight push, the door swung inward with a low moan, not unlike that of an irritated cat.

As a kid, he would have burst through the door throwing all caution to the wind and rushing into his grandmother's open arms. However, tonight he hesitated as the door came to a stop against the outside wall of the porch.

He turned on the flashlight and pointed it into the open doorway. As he moved the light around the room, a whole flood of emotions filled his heart. The boy in him wanted to run through the house yelling at the top of his lungs for those that were no longer there. The older man quietly took in the room in front of him cautiously.

Yes, there is where the ringer washer and wash basins used to stand. Over in that corner grandma hung her plants.

As the beam of light illuminated the room, Dan mentally checked off the locations of all the appliances that had once filled it.

He stepped cautiously into the room. As he completed the sweep with the flashlight, the light fell on a far corner. Two yellow dots glowed out of the shadows. He pointed the flashlights beam at the dots to get a better look. No sooner did the light fall on the area, than a dirty white feral cat let out a hiss and scrambled wildly to escape the room. Up it jumped to the far window sill and disappeared through a broken pane and out in to the night.

Caught off guard, Dan lurched back striking the door frame. For a moment, supported by the frame, he found himself back in Afghanistan looking in one of the many mud brick hovels with his unit. For a moment, as the adrenaline coursed through his body, he was ready to spring into action at any oncoming threat. He hadn't felt this jumpy in a long time.

Fortunately for the cat, he wasn't armed. He took a deep breath and pushed the thoughts out of his mind. It had been a long time ago and far away. "Steady", he whispered to himself as he swallowed back the anxiety that rushed up to consume him. "It was just a stinking cat."

Recovering quickly from his surprise, he let the beam of the flashlight again sweep around the room and then through the open door that lead to the kitchen. The kitchen seemed smaller than he remembered. Of course it would be, he thought. He had been a young boy the last time he had played here.

The cabinets still retained their white paint with red trim, but had dulled and been scratched over time. A small table sat just to the left of center of the room, where once his grandmother's dining table had filled the area almost to the exclusion of the chairs that had surrounded it.

In his mind he could envision the huge deep freeze that sat against one wall and the metal pantry that held up the opposite wall. The chirping of grandma's parakeet drew his mind's eye to a cage hung from the ceiling above the chest freezer. Grandma's voice chastising the bird rang in his thoughts. He mulled over the thoughts for a few moments, savoring the experience, until reality dissolved them away into the mists of memory, and he found himself staring at the now blank walls.

The table had a few old papers on it. With his flashlight, he rummaged through them. There were old pencil drawings along with soiled and coffee stained photo copies of blueprints for the construction of the new housing development.

As he moved around the table, his head bumped into a solitary light bulb hanging from the ceiling. *I wonder*, he thought to himself and reached up to the string that waved erratically in the air as the light rocked back and forth from the collision. A quick yank on the string, and the bulb came to life. It emitted a low yellow light that struggled to escape the bulb's dust and dirt covered surface to illuminate the room with an eerie glow. The shadows grew and shrank as the light continued to rock back and forth.

Dan reached up and steadied the light. He clicked off his flashlight, The old light fixture in the dining area had long been destroyed by vandals. In its place was a makeshift light that had been constructed from a length of old vacuum cleaner electrical cord and tied into the wires that remained from the old ceiling fixture in the main kitchen area.

He could hardly hold back a laugh as he traced the cord from the kitchen into the dining room. There it was, secured to the ceiling by two roofing nails that crisscrossed each other and held the cord with its solitary bulb suspended above the table. The length of cord was sporadically taped here and there to the ceiling with duct tape, the majority of which was slowly drying out and falling down. Some of his own adventures with electricity made him wonder if the craftsman who wired the project had a license. This looked like something *he* might jerry rig.

Dan moved into the living room. The dim light of the bulb filtered in behind him from the dining area. A long dark shadow stretched out in front of him along the floor. It moved ahead of him into the room and then blended in to the mass of shadows already occupying the space.

As Dan looked around, he could make out more construction supplies scattered around the room. Half used cans of plaster and paint sat useless, their liquids and binding agents evaporated away. An empty sixteen-penny nail box, half crushed, sat in the center of the room like a has-been prize fighter, waiting for someone to finish it off.

Gone were the old heavy living room chairs and sofa that had doubled as beds for him and his little sister. In those days, his parents would slide the two chairs together and make a bed for one, while the sofa would be folded out into another bed for the other. Now the room was just an empty cavity, devoid of warmth. Only the debris strewn about testified of its ever being occupied.

The grey light of evening crept in through the west window illuminating the space underneath. Where once his grandpa's television had sat, old used five gallon plastic buckets lay in a heap; their labels partially eaten away by mice and other vermin that had happened by looking for a meal.

In his memory, Dan could see his grandpa sitting two feet away from the TV trying to see as time's relentless march robbed him of his sight and his eyes grew dim. He could hear his distant, yet familiar laugh, as he slapped his knee over a joke told by the local weather man. The laugh seemed to ring louder in his mind as it reached out from the deep recesses of his memory, blending the past with the present and for a moment transported him back to his 12 year old self.

Good times, he thought, a tear pushing up into his eye, its progress arrested with a deep breath and a clearing of his throat.

Turning his flashlight on, he panned the room with its beam. In direct opposition to the traditions of the past, the front door on the north wall was closed and the deadbolt set. No more would a welcomed guest cross its threshold. Like the door on a tomb, it was sealed to the living.

Next to it was a window, still intact, but obscured by the build up of dust and dirt, the same grey evening light stealing its way through into open room.

Turning to his right, he looked into his grandparents' old bedroom. It was dark. The only light there was the light of the now rising moon as it poured in through the east window.

With flashlight in his hand, he slowly walked toward the room. Unfortunately, he didn't notice the pile of scraps on the floor in front of him and tripped. He kicked a chunk of wood that clattered across the floor and into the corner where the old coal furnace had stood.

The old coal furnace had been gone a long time; a very long time. Still it had always been a fascinating part of going to his grandparents' house. Before it was replaced with newer central heat, Dan had been given the opportunity to help his grandpa perform the daily chore of removing the 'clinkers' from the old furnace.

Clinkers were the melted together remains of metal and mineral impurities left over after the coal had burned away. It was his job to help fish them out of the furnace and carry them away to be disposed of in the trash barrel out back. Depending on the quality of the coal, the clinkers could be very numerous. The less expensive the coal, the more impurities were found and that made for more and bigger clinkers.

Dan remembered that on one occasion, early one morning, he had left the bucket next to the furnace while he ran to the bathroom. On returning, he had found his father sitting on the couch nursing a stubbed toe. Dad had not been happy with him. Chuckling to himself he headed into the master bedroom.

The room was empty except for a few Pepsi cans scattered about on the floor. Once, a large bed had occupied the west side of the room. Next to the far side of the bed had been grandpa's suit and dressing rack.

There had been mornings when Dan had entered the room and found grandpa sitting on his edge of the bed head bowed in prayer his hands resting on his lap. Quietly, Dan would back out into the living room and wait until he was done with his heavenly conference.

On another occasion he had found him sitting on his clothes rack stool wrapping his calves with ace bandages. Curious, he had asked his dad why grandpa did that. Dad had replied it was to help with his circulation and to alleviate the pain he felt as he walked. You would never have known grandpa was in pain when he came out. He would usually be hobbling along whistling a tune and ready to for his day.

A small walking area separated the rack from the clothes armoire that occupied the north wall. It wasn't as deep as a modern closet, but it was sufficient for their needs. Then again they didn't have a lot of fancy clothes either. Their life had been very simple, full of family and each other. Nothing else really mattered anyway.

On the east wall was the bedroom window. Under the window had been grandma's vanity, complete with her brushes and curlers for her hair.

Dan remembered a time when he had been called into the room and found grandma on her knees looking for a brush that had fallen from her vanity and been accidently kicked way back underneath. There she was, on her hands and knees, sweeping her hand under the vanity trying to reach the brush just out of reach.

Like a rescue ranger, Dan had crawled under the vanity and retrieved the wayward brush. Grandma had kissed him on the cheek and praised him for his heroics. Then she had ushered him into the kitchen to where the cookie jar sat. No better reward for a job 'well done' than one of grandma's home baked sugar cookies. Dan's mouth watered at the thought. Pavlov's dog had nothing on him, he mused.

Dan remembered that even though the room was small, it was a cozy room. Often at night, he would hear the elderly couple talking in the dark. Grandma would tell grandpa to roll over so he would stop snoring. Then she would roll over, and soon she would be sawing a few logs of her own. It was a droning chorus for the rest of the night.

In the morning, both would be up before dawn. Grandma in the kitchen dressed in her flower patterned dress, and grandpa poking away at the furnace with the stoker iron in his dark pants, suspenders and white t-shirt. Soon he would be off to the bathroom where he would shave and do his business, all the while whistling or singing a melodious ditty.

After looking around a moment longer, Dan walked through the small door that connected the master bedroom with another on the south wall. This was the room that his parents always stayed in when the family visited on leave. It had been the room where his aunts had grown up.

There had been a full size bed on the east wall, a dresser and an armoire that was full of papers, clothes, and treasured items. It was a small room, and the bed had filled most of it, leaving only a small walk way between it and the dresser that occupied the west wall.

The room had once been on the main thoroughfare for the grandkids as they had chased each other around in a circle through the house. Now it was empty and devoid of the substance that had given it life those many years ago.

However, as he listened, Dan could make out the faint echoes of the mourning doves' haunting songs as they filtered in from the south window early at morning's first light. A look out the window revealed the neatly kept garden out back. The mourning doves would congregate in the trees there to sing and coo.

A path led from the house to a little shack at the back of the garden. Its small door and window beckoned to the grandchildren, and it became the favorite place to play. It hadn't always been so.

As a youth, Dan's father had lived in the shack during the warmer months of the year. There had been a potbellied wood stove and a fold up bed inside. He had been relegated to the shack because the house was full of girls and the old shack had become his room, his domain.

Over the years, Dan had heard his father speak fondly of the little building and the nights he had spent there. After his dad had moved on, the shed had doubled as both storage and as an extra bedroom for the weary traveler.

By the time Dan had come along, the stove was gone, and the little shack was relegated to storage. However, the bed was still there, folded and secreted away in a corner.

When Dan's father retired, he had bought a bubble gum franchise from his brother in law. It was mostly to keep him busy. You see, after so many years of living in a world of giving and taking orders, dad had found himself lost in a world of civilian chaos. It was a world in which he never quite felt comfortable. The business was one way to be in command of his own time.

His organizational skills and flat out determination turned a small profit each month. It also required him to travel to eastern Idaho in order to service the machines once a month. It was a good opportunity to check in on the grandparents without looking like it.

23

On numerous occasions, Dan had gone along to help with the work. On one such trip, Dan had accompanied him to Idaho Falls. But because grandpa and grandma already had guests, the two of them had shared the shed for their room. They had slept in the old fold up bed. The mattress was thin, and by the end of the night, both had permanent kinks in their backs and sides.

On another trip, the two had awakened in the middle of the night choking on the horrid pungent smell of skunks. You see, behind the shack ran a ditch, and the local 'La Pews' would walk along it's bank spreading happiness to all who would breathe it in. But that was one of the hazards of walking merrily down the garden path and staying in the shack at the end. However, it beat sleeping on the floor in the house. For the most part, it had been a good time to be with his dad.

The door to the back porch was just outside that same south window. Anyone coming or going had a hard time escaping detection. Outside the window was the old coal shed. The shed was a small, dirty place. Inside was a pile of coal and an assortment of garden tools.

In the left corner, nearest the door, were the fishing rods and grandpa's fishing creel. The sound of the creaking door on the old shed signified that dad and grandpa were getting ready to go. An early morning rummage through the shed would produce the bait canteen full of night crawlers that the male members of the clan had stealthily extracted from the earth the night before.

The adrenaline and excitement would hit high pitch as the doors on grandpa's old, red 54 Merc slammed shut, and everybody was off to the hills for a day of fishing. By this time, the floods of memories were as tangible as cotton candy. Solid to the touch, but quickly dissolving with each bite, melting away with only the lingering taste to tell of the pleasure it had brought.

Dan shifted the flashlight's beam to his right and revealed another door that lead down a short hallway and back to the kitchen. The hall wasn't very long, at least not now. It had a gentle slope, and there had been a time when it had been ideal for the racing of his toy cars. He had had quite a collection of Matchbox brand cars and trucks. He loved to play with them on the gently sloping linoleum and watch as they picked up speed, finally spilling out into the kitchen. Mom and Grandma, on the other hand, weren't always as excited with his choice of venue; especially when they were trying to get supper ready.

And then there was the bathroom. The house had only one bathroom that grandpa had built when they put in the indoor plumbing. The only access point was in the hall.

Dan shined his light to the left and in through the bathroom's open door. The room was about the size of a medium-sized walk-in closet. The sliding door, that had allowed only a modicum of privacy, had been removed and was leaning against the north wall of the hall.

Through the opening Dan could see the old style wall sink where it hung on the west wall. The toilet was missing, leaving an open hole and the toilet flange in the floor.

Above, was a narrow window made up of about four or five glass blocks. Each block was hollow in the middle and measured about twelve inches in length, six inches tall and six inches thick. These allowed the daylight to shine in and illuminate the room from the south. At the same time their very thickness insulated the room from the cold of the Idaho winters.

The glass was recessed enough to allow for a small ledge or shelf that ran the length of the window. Dan could picture the plants and bathroom decorations that his grandmother had placed there to give the room atmosphere. Now there was only dirt and some kind of mold to line the shelf.

The old eagle claw bathtub, a relic of a different age when tubs were an experience not just another fixture, with its deep sweeping sides, sat on the left, just inside the door gathering dust. The porcelain that lined it was chipped and cracked revealing the rusting cast iron underneath. The tap and handles were rusty, the chrome long since cracked and dulled. Portions of the surface were encrusted with lime deposits from years of neglect and hard water build up.

Oddly enough, some of the chrome ball chain that had secured the rubber drain plug still hung stubbornly to its anchor under the tap. The plug had long since disappeared. Dried black and green mold had formed where the water had once dripped down from the overflow screen at the front of the tub. This formed a pathway to the drain where it merged with the rust stains circling the drain itself. It was all dried and hard now, the water having been turned off a long time before.

The sides of the tub were lined with a series of rusty rings that started about halfway up. The next ring was a few inches below the first. This pattern progressed down until they ran together at the bottom in a rusty, debris covered plain. It looked as if some ancient sea had evaporated over eons of time leaving only the rings as evidence of its existence.

To him it seemed such a waste. That old tub had been a great source of fun and adventure. Scores of naval battles had been won and lost in the vast expanse of that porcelain sea, not to mention the many scuba adventures conducted in its watery depths.

Once he had spent an entire evening in the old tub until every inch of his skinny eight year-old body was covered in wrinkles. When he got out he had stood on the cold linoleum floor, his teeth chattering, admiring his strange mutated skin. However, when mom had discovered his shivering form, she severely scolded him for being so stupid. But it mattered little to him. He saw it as a badge of honor and couldn't wait to share the tale with any who would listen.

What a thought, he recalled, as he turned his flashlight on the sink.

The sink, he observed, was in the same basic condition as the tub. The concentric rings, the mossy green progression down to the drain, the rust in the bottom; it all reflected the same degenerative condition that he had seen in the tub, only in miniature.

The door to the medicine cabinet that had once hung above, over the sink had been ripped off and the thin glass shelves that had held grandpa's shaving gear were mere shards of glass in the bottom.

Oddly enough, the old-fashion square light fixture was still mounted to the wall. The whole thing was composed of an opaque, white glass with a prism of clear crystal glass forming a circle on the bottom to illuminate the sink area below.

All of the pull chain, with the exception of about an inch-and-a-half, was missing, but otherwise the fixture was still intact, raising a fist of defiance and mocking the relentless march of time.

At 16 years of age, Dan had been asked by his grandmother to help his grandfather learn how to use the new Schick disposable razors. Grandpa had been using the same double edged razor for years, but with his failing eyesight had begun to have real bloodletting rituals every morning, and grandma was afraid for his life.

Grandpa was a proud man, and Dan had to use his best diplomatic skills to accomplish the job without hurting his feelings. He accomplished the task by distracting grandpa with questions about their favorite fishing holes.

While he and grandpa talked, Dan guided his hand to approximate the angle necessary to get a good shave. It didn't take grandpa long to get the hang of it, and Dan walked away feeling good inside. Now he looked down into the sink and marveled about the distance that had been crossed through time and how he missed his grandparents. *Some day,* he thought, *I'll see you again.*

An old hymn melodiously lilted through his mind. *'Til we meet, 'til we meet again,* it went on. He took a deep breath and once again choked back emotions that threatened to well up a second time. As he left the ravaged bathroom, he allowed only a solitary thought to cross his mind. *It's a far cry from the tidy bathroom that grandma insisted on.* The emotion was gone.

Out in the hall again, Dan lifted his flashlight to where he could view the top of the wall separating the bathroom from the hall. Yep, just as he had expected, it still didn't go all of the way to the ceiling. An eight inch gap separated the two.

He allowed himself a chuckle remembering that there was little privacy when one used the bathroom. Every sound that was produced within was free to wander on the breeze, over the wall, and out into the house.

And even more disconcerting was the fact that the door, a thin wooden sliding door, did not lock. It was always wise to let anyone around know that you were going to use the bathroom before doing so. Failure to do so could result in some embarrassing 'deer in the headlights' surprised situations and raised voices.

Sometimes it even paid dividends to wait till everyone had gone outside before doing your duty. At least then you could relax and were assured a modicum of self-respect; that is to say, no snickering from the kitchen. Of course, waiting too long could also result in some rather embarrassing situations to explain. It was a delicate balancing act.

His older brother had once given him a word of advice that was still paying dividends. He said, "He who hesitates is lost, so just go for it, and worry about the rest later." When it came to using the bathroom at grandpa's house, this was great advice. Dan had made note of it and always tried to remember that little boys had to be very careful and plan wisely.

His walk through the old house had brought him full circle and back to the kitchen. The old stove and refrigerator had been removed.

As he looked around, he could see that the kitchen sink was in the same condition as the bathroom fixtures. The house hadn't seen a kind hand in over 25 years. Every room had felt time's cold fingers curling and crushing all that had been virtuous and lovely out of it. Like a breath of warm air breathed out in the clear winter's night, its energy was spent, and only a fading cloud of mist marked its passing. The life that had sustained the house cooled and dissipated.

Once left to itself, time's icy lips drew out what remained.

Chapter 3

DAN WALKED OVER TO THE table where it sat under the light. Just beyond, in a corner by the kitchen's west window, he discovered an old metal folding chair hidden in the shadows. He took it from where it had obviously been shoved many years before and attempted to set it up.

At first it resisted his demands. But as he applied more pressure, the rusty hinges groaned deeply and then squealed to a high pitch as the chair gave way and unfolded. He set it down with a plunk next to the table. After wiping off the seat, he unceremoniously plopped himself down. He was tired. It had been a long day.

The light had quit swaying, and its soft glow had a tranquilizing effect; he felt the fatigue begin to set in. *I probably ought to get back to the hotel*, he thought.

Then, as if on cue, his stomach made a long gurgling sound, and he realized that he hadn't eaten since lunch earlier in the day. He reached into one of his jacket's many pockets and pulled out a small box. The writing on the box was plain and read, 'One Only Meal Ready to Eat—Chicken a la King.' It was one of his favorites.

The meal, or MRE, was one of several he kept in his car when he travelled. He had automatically shoved it in his pocket as he had parked the car for his trip. He reached into another pocket and pulled out a small plastic bottled water.

He cleared off a spot on the table, letting the old plans and papers fall to the floor. Opening the small box he neatly placed its contents on the table. There was a pouch full of the Chicken a la King, a small package with utensils, some gum, coffee, fruit drink mix, and a package of chemical for cooking the meal.

He picked up the chemical package and carefully cut along the indicated lines with his Swiss pocket knife he had retrieved from yet another pocket in his coat. That's what he loved about his military issued gear; there were pockets everywhere for everything under the sun.

Once the cutting was done he opened the bottled water and carefully poured a dribble of water into the chemical pouch. Neatly, he folded the top over to keep the contents from spilling out. Snipping open the top of the meal's main packet, he placed the closed chemical pouch in next to the "Chicken a la King's" inner packet. Now all he had to do was wait a few minutes and the meal would be hot and ready to eat.

As he set the whole assembly down on the table, he could feel the heat given off by the chemical pouch as it cooked the meal. Dan had done this so many times that he could do it in his sleep.

Like so many other things he'd learned in the army, this had become second nature, and he normally didn't give it a thought. However, tonight was different. Sitting in the dim light of the single bulb overhead, he found himself longing for Grandma's fresh green peas in cream gravy with red potatoes freshly dug from her garden. That was the meal that he loved the best.

After a day of bologna or peanut butter sandwiches, fending off blow flies with fingers that were grubby from bating hooks, Grandma's cooking was always the best way to end a day of fishing—not to mention that it was a lot healthier.

Fifteen minutes passed, and he reached over and pulled the inner meal packet out of the warming pouch. Carefully opening the meal, Dan took a quick sniff of the contents and let the aroma caress the olfactory processes deep within his nose.

He had always appreciated the effort that had gone into making the MREs palatable and had enjoyed the taste of the meals when out on patrol. But for some reason, this particular meal seemed extra good tonight in the old house. As he ate, he savored the taste. You would have thought he hadn't eaten in a week. But, of course, that would have been wrong.

Only a couple of days earlier, he had eaten dinner with his graduating class at the officer's club on the post at Fort Sill. The cooks there had prepared a mean prime rib dinner to celebrate the completion of the training cycle. After dinner, Dan had let out the waist band on his battle dress pants to be comfortable on the drive home. What a meal.

He scraped out the remaining bits of the MRE and, crumpling up the wrapper, stashed it in a dusty plastic Walmart bag he had spotted on the floor by the table's leg.

Rummaging around in the remaining contents of his MRE, he pulled out a peanut butter energy bar. This high calorie dessert was a far cry from its predecessors found in the old 'Meals Combat Individual' or C-rations as the Vietnam vet called them.

Dan's father had survived on C-rations in his years of combat and always had a small supply around for camping or fishing trips. Dan could remember his dad handing him a round C-ration can, about the size and shape of a tuna fish can. He then handed him a small tool that resembled a miniature scythe. The tool was about three inches long and had a sharp scythe-like piece that pivoted out at a right angle to the main piece or body. The tool was then employed as a can opener to open the military meals.

His dad had called it a p-38, and he always had one on his key chain. It was a handy little gadget once a person mastered its use. However, learning how to use it could result in frustration and often times drew blood from the uninitiated. As much as he admired the opener and his dad's adeptness with it, he was very grateful for the MREs and their ease of use.

Dan remembered opening the C-ration can and seeing the round 'hockey puck' pound cake inside. He had pried it out, a piece at a time, with his pocket knife. As he took a bite, the cake had crumbled in his mouth. It had an old musty cinnamon taste. The texture had been dry and it took a whole orange Nehi to choke it all down.

Like pouring flour into a cup of water, the liquid was seized upon and coagulated into a mouthful of semi dry paste. Still, his dad had assured him that it would be good. He swallowed it down with difficulty and tried not to let on that he wasn't enjoying it. It wasn't until years later that his dad told him he had watched with a chuckle as he had gagged it down.

With his meager meal eaten, Dan picked up his flashlight and walked towards the back door. The beam of light scurried on ahead of him and out onto the back porch.

Turning to his right he let the beam fall on the area where the cat had unexpectedly leapt from the corner and escaped out through the broken pane of the window. On the north wall that separated the porch from the kitchen hung the storage closets where grandma had stored her soaps, detergents, and other sundry products.

In one half was a tall area reserved for her old ironing board. The other half was lined with storage shelves. The nearest door of the cabinet hung open at a twenty-five degree angle, obscuring Dan's view of the inside. The other door was flat against the cabinet, its lower hinge broken. This had allowed the door to shift toward the outside far wall revealing a gap, out of which the cat had made his sudden dash to freedom.

A further sweep of the area revealed the large trap door recessed into the floor just in front of the cabinet. He traced the doors outline until he located the metal handle that was recessed into its surface. Reaching down he grasped the door and pulled up. Like the back door hinges, the hinges of trap door balked at his efforts and then gave way with a groan.

As the door swung upward his light revealed a set of wooden stairs descending down into the inky darkness of the cellar.

The cellar.

Yes, he remembered the cellar.

Chapter 4

THE THOUGHT OF HAVING TO go down there as a
boy was one that still sent chills down the back of
his neck.

Of course, it didn't help that his brothers had taken
great delight in telling him stories about the monsters that
lived down there.

It's funny, he thought, even after all the years that had
passed and all of the things he had experienced, the
thought of going down into that cellar still made him
shutter.

He chuckled to himself and then gingerly tested the
first of the old wooden steps. Like everything else in the
house, it creaked at the weight of his step. The flashlight

showed the stairs to be intact and in remarkably good shape.

Slowly he descended into the darkness, momentarily stopping as he remembered to duck his head as it nudged the washroom floor overhead.

The familiar smells of the cellar rose up to meet him. It was a musty, dank odor mixed with dust and dirt.

When he finally reached the bottom of the stairs, he swept the basement with the light. The old concrete walls greeted him like old friends.

His dad and grandpa had dug the old basement with pick and shovel, shoring up the floor above as they dug. They had poured the concrete walls and basement floor one bucket at a time, troweling by hand as they went.

The basement had been dug in the shape of an 'L'. The main floor ran west to east from the bottom of the stairs for about 20-25 feet and was approximately 14 feet wide. The portion of the basement directly under the stairs formed the leg of the 'L'.

At that point, the floor was raised up about 8 inches above the main area and measured approximately 10 feet deep back under the stairs, by 10 feet wide. It was back in there that Grandpa had made a small shop area where he stored his carpentry and other tools.

Along the south wall of the main floor and back along the wall under the stairs were shelves where grandma had stored her preserves and dried goods. She had also stored the folding chairs that were used for family gatherings deep in the corner back under the stairs. It was the catch-all place for storage. It was usually these chairs that Dan was sent to retrieve.

Instinctively, he waved his hand around in the air feeling for the old hanging light that, for years, had lit up the cellar. Pointing the flashlight to where he thought it should be, he watched as the beam reflected off the glass bulb hanging suspended in space.

Like the light in the bathroom, the pull chain had been broken off leaving only a few balls of the chain intact. Looking around the room Dan looked for a place to set the flashlight down so that he could have his hands free to reach for the light.

A space above the north wall caught his attention. When grandpa had dug the basement he had only excavated a portion of the space under the house. He had only dug out the space directly under the kitchen and the west section under the porch area. He finished by removing the earth directly under the girl's bedroom and the bathroom as well. As a result, the space under the living room and the master bedroom remained untouched.

Once the digging was done, grandpa and Dan's father had poured the basement floor and walls. A retaining wall was constructed to help shore up the dirt under the remaining portion of the house and give support to the floor above. This became the north wall in the basement.

It was very utilitarian in its construction and use. However, unlike the other three, the northern wall did not go all of the way up to meet the floor, but instead it only went up about three quarters of the way and had a gap of about 24-28 inches from the top of the wall to the bottom of the floor above.

Three strategically placed 6x6 posts rose out of the top of the wall and extended upwards to the floor joists at the bottom of the floor above, giving support. The remaining space was open to the view and you could see the dirt that had been under the house since its construction in the 30s. The beams that supported the floor travelled the length of the house from north to south creating wooden tunnels that lead away into dark places.

A person could see all the way back under the house. That was the realm of monsters and weird creatures. And for a little boy those many years ago, those recesses fueled his imagination, and he was apt to see eyes peering out from the darkness. This was again especially true if you had older siblings who took great joy in encouraging their little brother's fertile imaginations.

As Dan looked back into the darkness, he shook off a flash of the old dread that he had always felt after talking to his brothers. Scoffing at his silliness, he tried placing the flashlight on the edge of the wall. But because the top edge was rough and uneven, it wouldn't sit, but tumbled off instead.

Tucking the flashlight under his right arm, he reached up with his left hand and grasped the light at the cord. At the same time, he carefully reached up with his right.

No sooner did he reach than his light slipped out of his armpit and bounced off of his boot, skittering across the floor, its beam whirling around the room like a mad firefly.

This isn't going to work, he thought.

Retrieving the light, he looked around for something with which to prop it up. His gaze fell upon an old coffee can in a corner of the room. The can was full of old dried dirt and the remains of what resembled an old dead and dried tomato plant. Dan pulled out his knife and loosened up the soil in the can and then poked his flashlight, butt first, into the soil at an angle. He then positioned it so that the lights beam illuminated the basement ceiling around the hanging bulb. Satisfied with his inventiveness, Dan placed the can near where he needed to work.

Once again he reached up with his left hand and grasped the bulb, pinching and pulling the balls on the chain with the thumb and forefinger of his right hand.

With a reluctant click, the switch popped and the bulb burst to life illuminating the small cellar and momentarily blinding him. And though he had half expected the light to work, he was still startled when it came on and he inadvertently kicked the can containing his flashlight.

The can burst depositing the dirt all around and bouncing the flashlight on the floor with a thud where it half rolled to one side. The flashlight's unique 'L' shape halted its travel as it came to rest, the beam shining on the nearby wall.

Tough little light, he thought as he picked it up, turned it off, and clipped it to a keeper on his jacket.

The room was small and cool. It seemed as if no one had been down there in years. Strewn about the concrete floor were some old newspapers and a few empty cardboard boxes. The shelves along the walls had several old preserve bottles and cans.

Dan examined an old unopened can of green beans that was sitting on the shelf by itself. As he lifted it up, he noticed the circle indicating where the can had sat these long years.

The label was dusty, but otherwise intact. The jolly green giant was standing in a field grinning. As he looked at it, he noticed that it was slightly bulged at the top. *A little old and not so good*, he mused. He sat the can back on the shelf, being careful to put it exactly where it had been. The ring disappeared as the dust once again settled around the bottom.

As he moved around the room, his eyes were drawn to a faint line that ran around its circumference. It's still there, he thought. The line that marked how high the flood had gotten was still visible after all this time.

He remembered the story his father told about the
river flooding and the basement filling up. The family
had to dig up the slimy cold muck and carry it out in
buckets. It had been a favorite subject of his aunts when
the family recounted old stories and memories.

Everybody would gather around the kitchen table and
share their own interpretation of events. Grandma,
however, would sit on the high stool next to the stove and
listen. She would often have a bowl of peas in her lap.
And while she listened, she would shell the peas and grin
as grandpa narrated the stories of the old times. And
grandpa could tell a good tale, often slapping his knee
and laughing gregariously.

Now standing in the old cellar, Dan could almost hear
the sound of footsteps on the floor above. If he listened
close, he could make out the low murmurings of voices,
accentuated with bursts of laughter from a long-gone
relative whispering from the walls and floor boards.

Dan slowly made a 360 degree turn of the cellar
taking in all he could see. After a few minutes of
pondering, it was time to go. He headed for the stairs. As
he reached the light in the center of the room, he felt for
the chain. As he did, he glanced over toward the wall
beneath the stairs.

For a moment he thought he saw a glint of light just
under the steps. Squinting, he tried to see into the dark
corner but couldn't. He reached for his flashlight where it

hung on his coat. Snapping on the light, he focused its beam between the stair steps and into the corner. The light twinkled back, reflecting off what appeared to be a shiny surface.

Curious, he stepped up on the raised portion of the floor and peered around behind the stairs. In the corner was a pile of four ordinary bricks; the kind with three holes in them. He pointed his light up to the ceiling behind the stairway. Sure enough, the hole was still there. Another memory flashed through his mind.

The door to the cellar had become heavy as grandma had grown older, and it was difficult for her to lift it. One day when Dan, on a break from college, had come to see her, he had found her sitting in the living room looking despondent. When he asked her what was wrong, she had explained her frustration at not being able to get the trap door open.

Dan had a great love for his grandmother. She had been alone since grandpa had died and he knew she didn't like to ask for help. Seeing an opportunity to serve, he mulled the situation over in his mind. After examining the door, he hit upon a solution.

Gathering up several bricks, like the ones mentioned before, he rigged a pulley and a rope system to assist her as she lifted the door. Feeling excited, Dan called for his grandmother to come and try out the new and improved door.

Grandma shuffled into the porch where he stood smiling, very pleased with himself. At his encouragement, she bent down and gave the doors handle her usual tug. However, instead of resisting her attempt to lift, the doors swung quickly up and open, virtually on its own. Grandma had loaded up to make the lift and found herself thrown backward into the surprised arms of her grandson.

"Too much, huh?"

"Yes!" she had gasped out breathlessly. Still catching her breath, she shuffled into the kitchen and eased herself down in a waiting chair.

"I guess I used too much weight. I'll fix it, and we can try again."

After Dan had removed a couple of bricks from the lifting mechanism, they tried once more with a better result.

That had been a long time ago, and now, he found himself staring at those very same bricks stacked neatly in the dark corner.

He broke himself free and swept the area with his light.

It fell upon an object he had never expected to see.

Chapter 5

TUCKED AWAY ON AN OUT-of-the-way shelf, and hidden behind the stairs' descending support beam, was an old black telephone. You know the kind. The kind made of black Bakelite plastic.

There it sat with a wide round base that gradually narrowed as it rose to the top, its elegant shape reminiscent of a southern belle decked out in her ball gown. On the top rested the heavy black handset in a silver cradle, its shine masked under years of collected dust and basement dirt.

A thin black telephone cable wrapped in durable fabric insulation connected the handset to the base. Set into the base was a large rotary dial about four or five inches in diameter. At the center of the dial was a circle covered by a clear piece of plastic about an inch and a half in size. It's here that the home number was typed on paper and covered by the plastic cover.

Dan brushed off the dust on the cover and tried to discern what numbers were hidden underneath, but to no avail. Time had long ago obscured them. Along its perimeter, the dial had finger holes bored into it. Through each hole, a single number could be seen permanently affixed to the face of the phone. No matter how a person moved the dial, the numbers, like soldiers holding a defensive perimeter, never moved from their positions.

At the uttermost right edge of the dial was a silver half-moon finger-stop that overlapped the dial itself. In order to dial a number, a person lifted the handset with their left hand and then placed their index finger of their right hand into the appropriate hole with the desired number. They then rotated the dial to the right until it hit the silver stop. Pulling their finger out, the dial would rotate back to its original position. The person making the call would repeat this procedure until all of the digits in the telephone number had been dialed.

To end the call the person simply said goodbye and replaced the handset back into its cradle at the top of the phone. Phones of that time were very simple and straight forward. There were no cameras, texting, or internet connections. They were simply a tool for calling loved ones.

Dan set down his flashlight and picked up the phone. A length of cord, about twelve inches long, hung from its base and terminated in a frayed end. It had obviously been cut many years before to make way for a more modern incarnation of the communications device.

As Dan thought about it, he was sure he could remember several different phones in the old house as he had grown up. His grandparents had lived through the depression and, as amazed as he was to see the old phone after all of these years, he wasn't surprised that they had stored it away. Thrift and self-sufficiency had always accentuated their lives. "Waste not, want not."

It is quite a different generation from the one being raised today, he thought to himself.

The phone was quite a bit heavier than his little cell phone, but it just felt right, like a real phone. He lifted the handset with his right hand and with the phone in his left, clicked the receiver cradle up and down quickly with his left thumb. Unexpectedly, the light in the center of the room began to flicker and dim. Then, like a dying sun, it flashed brightly and went out.

Dan stood for a moment in the dark, allowing his eyes to adjust. The flash of the dying bulb had rendered him momentarily blind. Fortunately, Dan's flashlight was still on, and his eyes quickly adapted to the now somewhat dimmer source of illumination. Mentally, however, he noted that even the flashlight had grown fainter, and it seemed that it, too, would soon expire.

He picked it up from where it had sat perched on the wall and in its dimming light made his way to the stairs with his new found treasure.

As he ascended the stairs, he felt a slight rush of air brush by his leg as it rose up from the basement. At the time, he thought little of it and reached the top, stepping out into the porch. He felt like a free man as he turned and looked back down into the black abyss. The relief at having escaped the clutches of the basement monsters of his memory was palatable. *I guess it'll never leave me,* he thought.

Carefully, he closed the trapdoor and turned to the kitchen. No sooner had he turned than he heard the trap door lift an inch or so and then settle gently back into place with a light, but distinct thump.

Immediately his guard went up.

He spun around and quickly searched the area, half expecting to see something following him out of the basement. "Nothing."

He waited quietly, not moving, listening to the sounds around him. Not a sound but the creaking of the old house as it settled. "*Must be my imagination*," he chided himself.

Still he couldn't shake the feeling that something weird had just occurred. Warily, he took in the whole porch with his almost dead flashlight. It was still empty. He felt himself relax. The glow of the kitchen light shone in through the doorway, and he made his way back into the room.

Dan set the phone down on the table and dug through his jacket pocket for the spare set of batteries he always carried in the field. Finally, after a moment, he pulled out the new power packs and, unscrewing the flashlight's end cap, quickly replaced the dead hulks with the fresh batteries. With a push of the switch, the light came to life with renewed brilliance. Satisfied, he clicked off the light and set it down. He stuffed the old batteries into his pocket and again rummaged through his jacket for a candy bar he had stuffed there earlier. After a couple of tries, he located the elusive confectionary and extracted it from its hiding place with satisfaction.

Sitting down at the table, he opened the wrapper and bit off a mouthful of candy. *I looove Big Hunks*, he thought to himself. The white nugget stuck to his teeth, momentarily holding his mouth shut like glue. As he slowly chewed, the candy softened up and filled his mouth with the smooth vanilla flavor. He'd always loved the bar from childhood.

As he chewed, he looked the phone over. In the overhead light's soft glow, he could see the scratches that time and accidents had etched into its surface. Like the lines in a record, there was a message in each scratch.

What had happened in the past to cause the event to be engraved on the phone's black surface? He picked up the receiver and noticed that there were two relatively clean areas on the underside where it had rested in its cradle denying the dust lodging.

He wiped the receiver off with an old rag that had been lying on the table. At first glance, the wiping didn't seem to do much good, and it seemed for a time that he was wiping more dust on than off. The rag was just about as dusty as the phone, but with some pressure the chrome accents began to shine and the black surface to glisten.

Returning the receiver to its cradle, he proceeded to clean off the base. The dirt and grime had had plenty of time to set up and was stubbornly resisting his efforts. But with a bit of elbow grease and a few minutes of rubbing, the phone was somewhat presentable.

Dan kicked back in his chair with the satisfaction of a young recruit shining his first pair of boots and admired his handiwork. With little thought, he unwrapped the remainder of his candy and popped into his mouth. As he chewed, he admired the phone. Its simple elegance and utilitarian design fascinated him. There was no LED screen, no illuminated dials, and no texting pad. It was a simple, straight forward design. Dan again picked up the receiver and put it up to his ear. Somewhat sheepishly he glanced around the room to make sure he was really alone. When his "macho" was satisfied that it would not be compromised, he pretended to make a call.

Holding the receiver near his ear, but not too close, (it was still pretty dirty), he began to spin the dial. Five, two, six; with each number, he watched as the dial spun back to rest. Three, four; he pretended to listen as he spun the dial.

As he watched the next number return to zero, he became aware of a faint rhythmic sound issuing from the receiver's ear piece. At the same time, he noticed that as he dialed, the light began to flicker in rhythm with the clicking in the earpiece.

Dan stopped dialing for a moment. As if on cue, the sound and light stopped flickering. *That was weird,* he thought.

He looked around the room and waited to see if the power was going out. Nothing happened, and the room remained still, only the occasional sound of a car passing along the road out front.

Hmmm, he shrugged and passed it off as his imagination. Settling in again, he resumed tinkering with the phone.

No sooner did he begin to dial when the light again began to flicker. This time the light dimmed with an unmistakable rhythmic flicker and the pulsing sound in the receiver became more distinct. As soon as the dial reached the end of its rotation, the lights came back up and the pulsing ceased.

Now, the hair on the back of Dan's neck began to itch. A shiver crawled down his spine. Once again his survival instinct kicked in, and he became acutely aware of his surroundings. He knew he couldn't pass it off, something weird was happening. The very air around him felt charged, and his whole body felt as if millions of ants were crawling over its every inch.

Without hesitation, he leaned forward and unceremoniously slammed the receiver down on its cradle with a *bang!*

Instantly, everything was still and dead quiet. The light slowly built in intensity until it was back to its normal soft glow.

Dan became aware of the fact that he hadn't taken a breath since the whole phenomena had begun, and with a gasp, he sucked in a lungful of life-giving air.

What was that! he thought as he choked it down.

He stared at the phone, his hand still resting where he had slammed down the receiver.

Slowly, he withdrew.

His hand shook ever so slightly, and he swallowed hard to regain his composure.

He stared at the phone.

The last time he had experienced that kind of surprise was in Iraq.

Chapter 6

HE HAD BEEN RIDING IN a Humvee with his close friend, Cpt. Cedric P. Moser. They were travelling through Bagdad on their way north to the newly secured AL Quds Power Plant.

Their mission was to assess the damage inflicted by the nightly F-117 strikes at the beginning of Operation Iraqi Freedom. Cpt. Moser was a tall black man whom Dan had met on his first day in Officer's Candidate School (OCS) at Fort Benning, Georgia.

Moser was a member of the 19th Special Forces Unit based in Salt Lake City, Utah. He had been attending school at the University of Utah. Moser had graduated with a Bachelor's and later a Master's Degree in Engineering. He hailed from North Carolina, but had moved out to Utah hoping to walk on to the U of U's football team as a defensive end. When he hadn't made the team, he pursued his degree and joined the 19th to help pay for his tuition.

Upon graduation, he went on active duty, applied for OCS and was accepted. That's where he and Dan had met and been billeted together. When he found out that Dan had attended BYU, the old school rivalry sparked, and a keen friendship was born.

On completion of OCS, each had moved on to their respective units. In the intervening years, they had corresponded back and forth, crossing paths now and then during their careers.

When Dan arrived in Iraq, guess who was there to meet him? Cedric happened to be coming in from a patrol in the desert when he and Dan crossed paths at the Officer's Mess. After catching up on family, friends, football, and what was happening in the States, they had said their goodbyes, and Dan had headed out to his assignment. Just before leaving, Moser tossed Dan a taunt about how Utah was going to tromp the Y that year. Dan retorted, "In your dreams."

Cedric, with a big grin on his face, tossed Dan his special Ops knit cap and said, "Here. You're going to need this. It can get pretty cold in the desert at night. I'd hate to see that bald head of yours get frost bit."

"Look who's talking, Slick," Dan shot back. You see, Cedric always kept his head shaved.

With an even bigger grin, Cedric replied, "Keep it. I have two." Then he turned and briskly walked away.

"Catch you later," Dan smiled and waved goodbye as his friend disappeared through the door. He tucked the cap safely away.

It was a few months before the two met up again. They had been selected as part of a combined Ops teams and given the Al-Quds mission.

The team was travelling up Highway #2 on the northern outskirts of Baghdad when they had come under attack by Iraqi insurgents. Dan and Cedric were travelling together when a roadside IED exploded next to the Humvee, flipping it on its top. The explosion ripped the side of the vehicle open where Cedric was sitting, ejecting and killing him.

Dan had been shielded from the explosion by his friend and lay unconscious in the smoldering hulk. All that he could remember was waking up in a hospital bed with cuts, bruises, and an excruciating pounding in his head. His whole body ached and tingled constantly. Whenever he tried to move, a sharp shock of pain coursed through his six foot frame like someone was zapping him with a giant taser.

Miraculously, his injuries were not life threatening, and he only had to spend a couple of weeks in the hospital before returning to his unit.

The worst part was explaining to Tammy what had happened without giving out too much information. Her worried voice on the phone spoke volumes of their relationship. Like a cool compress on a severe sunburn, her voice had soothed his soul and gave him strength to move on.

Only Tammy could say how she felt after hearing him.

The army had awarded him the Purple Heart as a reminder of his experience. However, it did little to assuage the pain he felt, and still felt, at the loss of his friend. And for a time, even the eternal perspective couldn't quell the ache.

The news of Cedric's death weighed heavy on his heart. As soon as he could write, Dan wrote a letter to Cedric's wife, Nichelle, expressing his love and appreciation for her and Cedric. He told her of the last moments they had shared together and his deep sadness at his loss.

He felt compelled to take the time to express his beliefs in the resurrection and promises that the Lord has made to his children. In his letter, he bore his testimony and assured her that she would see Cedric again.

After he had returned to the states, Dan went to visit her. During that visit, they cried and laughed together as they remembered their good friend. They discussed important things concerning life, death, and that which brings eternal happiness.

When it was time to leave, Dan promised her that if she ever needed anything, all she had to do was call. Over the passing years, she had availed herself of his offer, often calling on him for help. And always good to his word, Dan, along with Tammy, would rush to her aid. However, as time passed, the requests became less and less frequent.

One day, a letter came in the mail. It was a wedding announcement proclaiming a new marriage for Nichelle. After several years of going it alone, she had found a friend to help her move on and close that chapter of her life. Not to forget, but to cherish, with all its experiences as teachers for the future.

From time to time Dan still received a holiday card or a short letter filling him in on her progress and thanking him for his being there.

Dan's physical wounds had healed quickly, but he never really got over the loss of his friend.

He reached up and touched the knit cap on his head, just to make sure it was still there.

Chapter 7

HIS SKIN HAD STOPPED CRAWLING and his thoughts had been returned to the present.

He sat staring at the phone.

What had just happened?

Without touching, he cautiously examined every inch of the phone looking for some clue to explain what he had just experienced.

I don't get it, he thought. *That's was really weird*.

After a moment he took a deep breath and tentatively picked it up again. Cradling it with both hands, he turned it over and examined the bottom. He wasn't quite sure what he was looking for.

In the back of his mind, he was hoping it was some kind of trick phone that someone had left behind as a prank. However, the bottom was flat and covered with the old dark green felt that had been prevalent in its day.

What did you expect to find? he chided himself silently.

He sat the phone down, leaned back in the chair, and just stared. After a few minutes, he picked up the receiver and again placed it next to his ear.

After a moment of hesitation, he slowly began to dial and, as before, with the release of the dial, a distinct clicking sound emanated from the handset.

Again on cue, the light overhead dimmed and pulsated with the rhythm of the dial winding down. Dan rotated the dial a second time. This time the effect became more pronounced and, again, it stopped as the dial came to rest.

He looked around the room for a moment and then dialed a third time. Instantly, the room flickered, and the ear piece clicked. However, as the dial came to rest, the light surged bright and then dimmed sharply to almost a flutter.

Dan looked up to see the bulb's filament barely glowing. The room was plunged into darkness as the light bulb suddenly flashed brightly and exploded showering glass all over. Dan instinctively covered his face with his arms.

The room fell silent, and he sat nervously in the dark. Beads of sweat ran down his cheek. He gazed forcefully into the dark, every sense reaching out for an explanation or a cause.

Nothing...

Again...nothing.

He became aware of his pulse pounding in his ears. He swallowed cautiously and listened. *What is going on,* his thoughts raced.

Presently, he became aware of a voice.

"Who's there," it asked?

The voice was extremely faint and muffled.

"Where is *that* coming from?" Dan whispered under his breath. In the dark, he felt around the table for his flashlight. Bumping it with his hand, Dan located the switch and turned it on.

"Hello? Who's there?" asked the voice.

Shining his light around the room, he searched for the source of the sound. He became aware that he had dropped the receiver, and now, it was dangling suspended over the edge of the table. As he reached over and pulled it up by the cord, he was startled to realize that the voice was emanating from the receiver itself.

Cautiously he raised the phone to his ear. "He-hello?" he said.

"Who is this?" the voice questioned rudely. "I have the line right now, and I don't appreciate you eaves dropping on my phone calls."

The voice was that of an elderly woman, and it was laced with indignation. Flabbergasted, Dan held the receiver at arm's length, staring at it incredulously. This had to be a trick. But who was playing it?

He put the phone back to his ear and quietly listened. The voice began talking about the events of the day. Dan suddenly became aware that there was another woman on the line with whom the first was conversing. This was now getting more than bizarre, and he couldn't believe what he was hearing.

As he listened, somewhat self-consciously, another voice began to whisper, almost imperceptibly, in the back of his mind. With each word, the voice on the phone—and the one now growing in volume in his mind—seemed to blend into one. The voice, now clearly one, was strangely familiar. "Where on earth have I heard that voice before?" he questioned.

"I'm not sure where I'm going to find that brand of bulb today. I dug up last year's bulbs and had Dad put them away in the shed for the winter, and now I can't find them."

Dan couldn't quite make out the voice on the other end of the phone, but whoever it was must have asked about Dad's whereabouts.

"He's gone off fishing with Jasper and won't be home till dark, and it's the perfect day to plant," the first woman replied. "Sometimes that man can be so frustrating," she vented. "If I'm going to have my Gladiola's ready for the fair, I'm going to have to buy some 'store bought' bulbs, and you know as well as I, that if you don't grow them yourself, you can't be sure what your goanna get."

The other woman was saying something, but it was inaudible to Dan. He had already stopped listening. Gladiola's? Fishing? Jasper?

He milled the words over in his mind. Normally, he wasn't easily shaken, but the phone, the voices, and now this conversation was making his skin crawl again.

He had heard those words before, and he had heard them spoken by the now all-too-familiar voice. The voice he was hearing was that of his own grandmother—gone many years hence!

That's impossible, he argued to himself.

Yet, there it was, the voice on a phone that wasn't connected to anything, in an abandoned house slated for demolition.

He fought the urge to flee.

Everything he had learned and experienced in his life told him to get out. And yet, deep inside, another voice— a quiet voice—filtered through the fog whispering that everything would be alright.

Mentally, he grabbed and held on. A quiet calm enfolded his whole body like a warm blanket, and his anxiety melted away. He had learned long ago to trust that little voice. In his darkest hours, it had never failed him. A tear welled up in his eye, and he quietly whispered a *thank you* into the dark.

Still uncertain of what to think, he slowly set the handset down on the receiver and sat silent in the dark, pondering the events that had passed.

Picking up his flashlight he made his way to the back door. Stepping out into the night, he paused. The rain had subsided, and a patch of sky shone through where the clouds had parted. As if the curtains of heaven were drawn back, the night sky glistened with numberless points of light that were stars in procession. The moon shone on the clouds like back lighting on a stage curtain during a play.

As the clouds moved on the winds, the scene changed revealing more stars and glowing planets. In the dim light, he could make out the outline of the little shed at the rear edge of the property. Dan took all of it in and realized that it had been a long time since he had stopped and appreciated God's creations as he did tonight.

After watching nature's display for some time, he walked to the back of his car and opened the trunk. He clicked off his flashlight and hung it back on his jacket as the trunk light once again lit up the interior of the trunk.

After rummaging around for a few seconds, he found what he was looking for. Lodged down in the well that had once housed the inflatable donut tire, it being discarded long ago in favor of a real tire in the trunk, was an old gift he had received several years ago from his mother at Christmas.

The box was tattered and torn, but intact. Inside was a battery powered lantern, the kind that has the flashlight, lantern, and blinking caution light built in. It also had a handy-dandy combination space blanket/poncho in a small pouch on the carrying sling.

The whole thing had been his father's and had seen a lot of miles in the old station wagon as the family had crisscrossed the country from one posting to the next. After dad had died, it had been stashed away in the garage at the old house with much of his car stuff.

When the house got too big for Mom to manage, Dad's things were handed out to Dan and his siblings. Now after so many years and vehicles, the lamp was finally going to be used. After a little more fishing around in his emergency supplies, he located some batteries.

Taking the lamp out of the box, he slipped the batteries inside through the door in the bottom. Flipping the switch, the lamp came to life. It cast a blue-white light on the ground as the fluorescent bulb warmed and glowed. Dan closed the trunk and walked back into the house.

The lantern cast its blue-white glow on the walls and sent the shadows fleeing away into the recesses of the cracks between the wooden boards that made up the floor. The glow slid along the now tattered and dirty linoleum that had once sported a beautiful high gloss shine. No more did the heart that once filled the home see to its weekly cleaning and polishing.

The dust again rose and settled as Dan made his way back to the table. Sitting the lantern on the table, he plunked himself down in the chair. No sooner had his butt touched the seat, when the phone let out a series of loud rings.

Caught off guard, Dan jumped up and stood staring once again at the ominous black object on the table. The phone let out another series of rings and was silent. Again, a third time, the rings filled the room. Dan jerked the receiver off the cradle and breathlessly answered, "Hello?"

A women's voice timidly asked if this was where she could get a load of manure delivered to her home for her garden. Dan started to say something when he realized that someone else was on the line. However, this voice was different. The voice was that of a man. This time it didn't take a tree falling on him for him to realize that the voice was that of his own grandfather.

Now over the initial shell shock of hearing his grandma's voice, and realizing that something real, albeit impossible, was taking place, a wave of excitement surged through him.

"Grandpa!" he choked out excitedly. "Grandpa!"

The voice on the phone continued without missing a beat. "No, I'm afraid you called the wrong number. You want this number...." He rattled off a number. "The stock yard phone number is the same as ours, except for the prefix," he explained.

"Oh dear, I'm so sorry," the woman panicked apologetically. "Thank you," she said embarrassed, and then there was a click. The man let out a chuckle, and then click, the line fell silent.

Impossible as it had been, Dan couldn't deny that the man's voice was that of his beloved grandfather. He had died some thirty-three years before.

His mind rolled back to the flight home.

He had less than two weeks left on his mission when the call had come. When the choice to stay or come home had been laid in his lap, he had agonized for a couple of hours. The decision to return home and be with his family, in particular his own dad had seemed so clear.

His dad had been inactive for years, and Dan felt it was important to support him in his hour of need. His mission president had supported his decision and had had the assistants' book a flight home for him that evening.

With only a few hours to get ready, Dan had gathered his stuff and made the obligatory souvenir trip to the local market. As the evening fell, he had dinner with the president and his wife and soon was on the flight home.

Flying through the night, he had a lot of time to contemplate those two years in the Lord's service. He hadn't been expected to fill a mission as he grew up, like many of his companions, but he did his best to learn and to do. It had been hard, but rewarding. He had learned how to motivate himself when everything around him was telling him that it was no use. It had been a personal battle to love the work and the people.

Had he been a good missionary or merely done his time? He wrestled with his conscience for some time. Was he doing the right thing going home early? Was the Lord pleased with his service?

From time to time, and for many years later, that question would pop up in times of self doubt. Then, as if to answer, something would happen to confirm to him that he had succeeded in spite of it all.

However, at that moment in time, as the flight had continued, the excitement of going home had overcome his doubts. He knew he was needed and felt an urgency to get home before his grandfather passed.

When he finally landed at his hometown airport and embraced his mother for the first time in two years, he learned that his grandfather had passed while he was yet in flight over the Pacific Ocean. Glad as he was to be home, Dan's heart was sad to have missed him.

Reality slowly pushed its way into his thoughts.

He became aware that he was listening to a dead phone. The call was gone.

Dan sought, but couldn't find an explanation for anything. He looked at his watch. Seven o'clock. The evening was still young. He became aware of the rain beating upon the house. As the wind picked up, the intensity increased. The rain hammered at the windows threatening to break through.

It reminded him of intense small arms fire against the armor sides of the old M113's. The old personnel carriers' thin armor had also threatened to give at times under the furious onslaughts of the enemy. As the thought crossed his mind, he could feel his pulse increase.

"Steady boy," he whispered under his breath. He felt himself relax.

Ring! Ring!..... Ring! Ring!

The phone came to life, the handset still in his hand. By this time, he was getting used to surprises. He put the receiver to his ear.

"Hello?" he spoke into the mouthpiece.

"Hello, mother!" a young woman's voice cheerfully greeted.

No sooner did he begin to reply when the voice he recognized as his grandmother's replied, "Why, hello dear. Isn't this a pleasant surprise."

"I told you when I got to work, I would call you and check in," replied the young woman. "I'm learning a lot about the telephone business working here. Hold on, Mother. I have to switch another call."

There was a moment of silence as the young girl went off line for a moment. With a click, the girl was back.

"Did you hear that they're going to ration meat, cheese, and butter? They say it's to help the troops who are fighting overseas. It's a good thing we have enough seeds to plant the garden again this year. It sounds like were going to need it. Mable says that her friend, June, told her that some government official just announced it on the radio. You ought to go turn it on. I just wish they'd have killed old Adolf in that bunker last week. Maybe the war would be over and our boys could come home."

"Hey! Are you two gonna yak all day?" The voice had a high-pitched, nasally quality to it. "Some of the rest of us need to make a call."

"Don't get your bloomers in a bunch, Gladys. A person can't be on the phone two minutes, and you got some sort of an emergency you have to use it for. You can wait till we're done," Grandma quipped back.

Gladys, as Dan remembered her, was the nosey neighbor up the road. He had only heard her in her advanced years. However, her voice sounded just as annoying now as it had when she had chewed him out the first time as a youth. The only real difference was that as he heard her now, her voice was more robust and piercing.

"Well, I never!" Gladys huffed and slammed down the phone with a *click*.

"I guess I better go, Mother. I suspect I'll be getting a call soon from a concerned customer," the young girl chuckled.

"Okay, dear," Grandma acknowledged with a snicker. "Oh, and Mary—call if you're gonna be late so I can save you some supper."

"Alright, Mother. Good-bye." With that, the line went dead.

Mary, Dan mused. *Aunt Mary? Wow!*

Several years previous, Dan and Tammy had been out for an afternoon drive in the country when they happened to drive past an old dilapidated one-room school house. They began discussing who might have gone to the school and what stories it could tell, if only it could talk. What secrets were wound up in the folds of the peeling paint and sagging wallpaper? Dan had often heard people say, 'Oh what stories these walls could tell.'

Walls? Dan thought. *Who needs walls? I've got an old, disconnected telephone, in an old, soon-to-be destroyed house, bringing me the conversations of dead relatives as if they were occurring right now. Now that's what I call signal strength. The cell phone companies would be jealous.* "Can you hear me now?" Dan shouted into the mouthpiece. The phone remained quiet.

This is all a dream, and I'm going to wake up and find myself in the officer's billet, face down, drooling on my pillow.

Dan stood and pensively walked around the table trying to make sense of it all. Another person would have left at the first flickering of the lights. But not Dan. It took a lot to get him rattled. Either he was extremely brave or nuts. "Nuts," he commented to the silent room. However, he had to admit that even if it was a bit unnerving, it was too much to simply ignore. And now it had his full attention.

Circling the table, Dan awaited the next ring. He didn't have long to wait. The phone sprang to life in a long constant *rrrrrrriiiinnnng!* The vibration caused it to move eerily about the table. Dan watched, transfixed on the strange scene. The ringing stopped abruptly for only a fraction of a second and then ripped off another round of sound while vibrating around the table top. Dan grabbed for the receiver, snagging it and the phone's body as it slipped off of the edge.

He pressed the receiver to his ear. The voice was that of a man.

"He's been up on Homer Creek tending to the sheep," the voice said. "He's been up there all week. I'm going up to bring him home this afternoon. I thought we'd fish a little before the sun sets."

The familiar, voice made his heart beat faster, as if it wasn't racing fast enough.

Grandpa!

Chapter 8

A<small>S HE LISTENED, HE BECAME</small> aware of a low gray light. He looked around to determine where it was coming from.

As the light increased, ever so slightly, the bulb in the center of the room faded to almost nothing. Only the wire filament's low orange glow indicated that it hadn't been extinguished. Looking around, he discovered the walls in the room were emitting the strange gray light.

The light grew until, like an old black and white television, the walls came to life. As he watched, he began to make out the outline of a short, stout man with a phantom phone. The phone just like the one Dan himself was holding. And like Dan's phone, there was no cord attached.

The particles of the outline coalesced until a ghostly apparition stood before him holding and speaking into the phone.

"Grandpa?" Dan gasped to himself. In stunned silence, he watched the ghost move around the room. As its lips moved and the sound filtered out of the phone clutched in Dan's white knuckled hand, he watched, the dust on the floor rising up and merging. The ghostly apparition morphed from the two dimensional image on the wall into that of a three dimensional being standing in the room.

Grandpa walked into the living room, still holding and talking into the ghostly phone. As he did so, the light around him seemed to slide along the wall as if a giant projector were being turned from Dan's view.

As the apparition disappeared into the living room, Dan stood alone in a darkened kitchen. All of this time, Dan had stood immovable watching as the specter moved happily without even a sideward glance at him.

Cautiously, he commanded his legs to move toward the doorway that divided the kitchen from the living room. Peering through the opening, he could see the same eerie light emanating from the walls, illuminating the living room. Dan peered further around the corner to where Grandpa sat in a now phantom easy chair. He continued to laugh and talk into the phone. Dan had let the receiver fall to his side. He silently lifted it to his ear.

"You know ole Jasper loves to fish up there. He loves to fish so much that he takes off without a thought—and without his bait canteen.

"One time, he got all of the way up to Brockman and had to dig up night crawlers right out of the bank. Since he didn't have anything to carry them in, he just stuffed them in his pocket. When he got home, he tossed his pants in the laundry. Funny thing is that he'd forgotten to take them ole night crawler out of his pocket. The next day, when his wife was fixing to wash his pants, she found them. She was pretty mad. I was sure glad I wasn't Jasper that day. She gave him quite a scolding." Grandpa gave a hearty chuckle, at the same time, slapping his knee. Grandpa's chuckle faded to silence, and his image dissolved like smoke being blown before a small, gentle breeze.

The gray light gathered itself on the west wall of the living room and slipped slowly along the wall until it reached the corner, next to the door of the kitchen where Dan stood. Motionless, Dan watched as the light and dust rose from the floor and once again congealed, first on the wall, and then into another three dimensional figure.

Three feet away from him stood another ghost. The image was that of a woman in her early sixties, her hair short and tidy. She wore a light colored dress covered with small flowers. Her back was to him, and she seemed to be dusting or cleaning a phantom shelf that had once occupied the corner. She shuffled ghostly knick knacks back and forth as she dutifully cleaned.

Dan hung up the receiver quietly back in its cradle. Suddenly and without warning, the figure turned and walked straight at him. Caught off guard, he instinctively braced himself for impact. Without even a wisp of air, the phantom passed right through him and turned into the kitchen, the dust separating and then reconstituting itself, the specter ignoring him as if he was not even there. Gathering his wits, Dan cautiously followed a few feet behind.

When he entered the kitchen, the woman sat perched on a white step stool. In her lap rested a large ceramic bowl. She sat with her head down, silently working with something in the bowl.

As he drew nearer, Dan could see that the bowl was full of fresh picked peas. The light came on in his head. Here was Grandma, a little younger than he had last known her.

Watching her work the shells without much effort spurred thoughts of summers spent at the old house. He remembered the warm summer days and the big garden that she so lovingly kept. In one section were the vegetables for eating and canning. In the other were the rows of Gladiolas she grew to perfection.

In his mind, he could see and hear the bees as they busily flew from flower to flower collecting nectar and pollen. Many times when the family had visited, he would accompany Grandma out to the garden to dig up something for dinner. A favorite were the red potatoes. He would carefully dig down and turn over the rich soil to reveal the potatoes. After a few minutes of digging they would have filled a bowl with the treasure trove of spuds.

Next he would help her pick and shuck the fresh peas that grew prolifically throughout the garden. Later that night, Grandma would transform the haul into a heavenly dinner of fresh potatoes and peas in creamy white gravy. The dinner would have all of the trimmings, including fresh canned peaches and cream.

He stood watching.

She looked up from her work and straight into Dan's eyes.

He felt himself stiffen.

She smiled softly and went back to her work.

How strange, he thought. Here I am in an old house, listening to a phone that hasn't worked in over forty years, and now I have ghosts smiling at me. What's next?

RRRRRIIINNG!

The phone came to life in his hand, but now he had grown used to it and didn't jump. He glanced up at his grandma just in time to see her disappear, a kind smile on her face.

Dan held up the receiver and listened.

"When are they supposed to be here?" asked an unseen woman. "We're going to need a couple of tables from over at the church, and we want to be ready when they get here," she said.

"Doug said that they would leave Fort Benning on Tuesday. So let's see, that should put them here Friday night," answered another younger girl.

Dan moved to where he could peer once again into the living room. The ghost of Grandma now sat in her easy chair doing needle point. The apparition of Grandpa was parked in another chair bent forward about three feet in front of a large console TV set that had materialized and once again occupied the west wall under the window. Grandpa gazed intently watching a man dressed in a suit, reminiscent of the mid 60's styles, announcing the weather. Every so often, he would let go a hearty laugh as the weather man said something he found funny. Dan watched, from where he stood, transfixed on the scene.

In the north east corner of the room sat a young woman talking on the phone. Even though her voice was low, he could make out bits and pieces of the conversation over the phone receiver. The girl was in her mid-twenties and was busy talking about arrangements for some big party that was going to take place later in the week.

As Dan watched, he realized that the young girl was his own Aunt Lidia. She had served a mission in the

South Pacific just as he had. He always had a soft spot for her and her quiet determination. His own sister was a close copy of all the good things that Aunt Lidia possessed. They were two very determined and righteous women.

Lidia finished talking to the caller on the phone and got up from the couch. She walked past Dan, into the kitchen, and up the hall, past the bathroom and disappeared into her bedroom. He turned and watched her as she closed the door softly behind her.

No sooner had the door closed than it disappeared in a whirling wisp, leaving the now darkened opening of the abandoned room. The dust lay undisturbed on the floor except for where Dan's tracks revealed his first passing.

He looked back into the living room. It was also empty now, the only signs of life being the occasional flicker of lights filtering in through the windows from the road as the cars sped past. The headlights cast eerie shadows that raced across the walls like demons fleeing heaven's light.

Gone were the images of family; still was the dust.

The phone was silent.

Chapter 9

DAN STOOD PEERING INTO THE empty room. Darkness had once again taken hold, and an empty hollow feeling filled his soul. A longing for those gone or distant washing through his soul.

Memories of people and events flooded onto the stage of his mind. Yet every time he tried to focus on one, it would fade back into the background and another one would burst onto the scene.

People, places, and things filled his mind with wonder, threatening to overwhelm him. He shook his head vigorously trying to clear it.

In an instant, the clutter was gone, and he was alone in the darkness of the house.

He walked over to the table and sat down. He sat the phone down on the table. He felt like an old wrung out wash rag.

He wondered if he had somehow bumped his head while he was down in the basement.

No, I would still be down there passed out if I had hit it that hard, he assured himself.

Maybe I ate a rotten 'Big Hunk', he mused. *No, not possible,* he abruptly banished the thought as ludicrous.

What then? he questioned.

By now, his head was beginning to clear, and he began to notice that the light had returned and was starting to brighten. It cast a soft, friendly glow around the room. It was emanating from the kitchen, from where the light hung silently in the center of the room.

He looked up and noted the light's shattered form and realized that it was impossible. The light had burst when everything had begun happening. It should be out, and yet it was getting brighter.

He watched, amazed as the dust began to scurry across the floor. It swirled and danced about three inches above the old linoleum. As it danced, the walls again glowed with the strange gray light that had illuminated them before. Dan sat looking around, transfixed by the scene. Slowly, ever so perceptively, the dust rose and swirled combining with the gray light and congealing like a caramel batter in a slow moving mixer. As the elements combined, it flowed out from its center to touch the walls and form objects.

First the cabinets began to form, and then furniture rose out of the now giant swirling, wondrous mass. The table where Dan sat changed, elongated, and transformed into a large dining table. The kitchen was changing rapidly, and the whole of the house was going through a strange metamorphosis. All about him, the home was changing, changing into something new, yet very familiar.

All of Dan's senses were afire. He wanted to run or fight, but the wonder of it all nailed him to his seat.

At the same time, something inside was softly whispering, *"Be still, all is well."* As the voice became clearer, he found himself relaxing, a feeling of peace resting on his mind. It was that feeling he had felt so many times as a missionary in the South Pacific and as a young soldier in combat in the Middle East.

The scene continued to grow. Tables formed end to end, starting in the living room at the front door and continued through the kitchen to the back door. On the tables were white linen table cloths and beautiful centerpieces.

Foods of every kind appeared on the tables. Turkey, potatoes, yams, homemade rolls, and jams of every variety distributed evenly along the line. Of course, there were plenty of olives to go around.

Pitchers of drink were placed here and there every so often, along with other home canned preserves. The ghostly feast was like a pencil drawing of grey and white formed in ghostly outline. Like an architect's drawing everything was there, but there was no physical substance, and was devoid of color.

There it was, the whole house sketched out as it had been when his grandparents had occupied it. Dan reached out to touch the table. His hand passed through it as if it were air. The phone rested on the plain that was the table's surface, seemingly supported by some unseen hand. The silent commotion, for it had all occurred in relative silence, had begun to settle. The dust was gone and only the glistening strands of elements outlining the now remade home's interior remained suspended in position as if awaiting the final act of the divine.

Cautiously, Dan stood and walked around. He passed through the strands that glistened and glowed with the strange light. It was like walking through a drawing. In perfect detail, it was all there, right down to the old clock on the wall.

As he walked, he became aware of a low hum that was beginning to fill the home. Slowly, it rose in volume. Even though he wondered what it could be, he felt no fear.

As he cast his eyes about to see where it was coming from, his attention was drawn to the front door where a figure began to take shape. At first, it was but a figure with little to no features. However, as he watched, its features became sharper and more familiar. It strolled into the room as if coming in from outside.

"Uncle Rod?" Dan gasped.

There he was in his businessman's suit and hat, a smile on his face. From behind, Dan could hear voices, and he turned to see several people coming in the back door from the porch. They were talking and laughing as they filed in.

Aunt Lidia and her sisters were talking with Sharon, Aunt Lidia's old mission companion. Sharon had come to the states to attend college after her mission and had become another member of the family. Even after she had married and moved away, she tried to attend as many of the family functions as she could. Dan saw several of his cousins with which he had romped as a boy. They were all young, about ten to eleven years old, and they ran through the house at break-neck speed with only the indignant reproach of the older members to slow them.

Grandpa had just entered the living room from somewhere and was talking to Uncle Jack who had come up from Pocatello, Idaho, with Aunt Mary. Aunt Mary and Uncle Jack had met and married just after he had got home from serving in the Pacific Theatre during WWII.

They had run a small Italian café down in Pocatello for a number of years while raising their family. Every time Dan and his family would stop in to see them at the cafe, Uncle Jack would give him a couple pieces of beef jerky from his private stash and an orange Nehi to wash it all down. That was a treat he had always looked forward to.

Standing nearby was Uncle Darren. He had been a school teacher in Teton, Idaho. He had married Aunt Mable, Dan's father's little sister. They always brought the family down from the mountains for every family get together they could. The snow of winter was about the only thing that could stop them, and only if it was deep enough.

Aunt Mable had passed away only a few years ago, and Dan taken had leave to attend her funeral. It had been a sad day, and he missed seeing her. Uncle Darren was having a good laugh with Aunt Lisa, another one of his aunts and the stalwart of the family. She was married to Uncle Rod. She lived the closest and was always looking out for Grandpa and Grandma.

When Dan's family came home on leave, Aunt Lisa was one of the first to come over and greet them. Dan liked to go and spend time at her house and would do so throughout his life as he passed through town. She would never know how much she meant to him and his own family.

As Dan watched the spectacle unfold, he found himself caught up in the whole affair, just as he had been as a boy those many years ago.

The hum in the room had grown to a dull roar. There was something about the hum that drew his attention. As he focused and listened, he began to make out words. Soon the hum began to separate into distinct and very familiar voices. The room was awash with the conversations of the various ghosts as they walked about the house. Their voices now audible, continued to grow louder and louder until he thought his head was going to burst.

He threw his hands over his ears and promptly realized that the voices were in his head. No sooner did he cover his ears than there was another bright, almost blinding burst of light. He closed his eyes against the flash while still holding his ears.

As the flash subsided, he opened his eyes to see the room filled with relatives. The room was also filled with colors, the colors of his grandparents' home as it had been in his youth. The cabinets appeared solid with the light grey marbled tops splashed with tiny specks like pepper. The borders were outlined in red and topped off with chrome or silver trim.

The living room was alive with vibrant color from the drapes to the carpet. The hum had now passed, replaced by the conversations of a joyful household. Dan scanned the room in wonderment. The people all looked real, not like before, and Dan had to wonder what had changed.

Tentatively, he reached out to the table nearest him and touched it. It was solid. He ran his hand over its closest edge. Astonished, he whispered to himself in disbelief, "It's real!"

All of the family assembled around the tables and bowed their heads as Uncle Darren was asked to pronounce a blessing on the food. Reverently, he bowed his head and very humbly thanked Heavenly Father for all they had been given. He expressed a desire for each to be blessed with their needs and with a grateful heart.

After closing the prayer, each of the family grabbed a plate and began to dish up their food. Instantly, Dan became aware of the smells of the freshly cooked foods. The room was filled with the aroma of freshly roasted turkey and ham. The smell of fresh baked rolls greeted Dan's nostrils with pleasure, making his mouth water. Where once there had been only outlines and black-on-white imagery, now there was substance and color.

Dan watched quietly.

Suddenly, an excited shout rang out from the living room, "They're here! They just drove in!"

Dan couldn't make out who was yelling, or for that matter, who they were shouting about, but it filled the air with even more excitement.

The sound of gravel crunching under a car's tire could be heard out in the driveway. Several of the children ran to the back door, and those who weren't eating followed close behind.

Who could it be? Dan wondered. *Who was missing?*

Grandma, who had been dishing out potatoes in the kitchen, untied her apron and headed for the door with Grandpa falling in step behind.

Dan could hear happy and excited voices coming from the porch. He could hear the noise of backs being slapped and children running into the house. Several children burst into the kitchen and sped on to the living room. Three of the children looked very familiar to him, but they moved so fast that he had hardly had a chance to glance at them. Besides, his attention was drawn to the back porch and the wad of people returning to the kitchen.

"We expected you last night. We were worried you wouldn't make it," said Grandma.

"I'm glad you all made it," greeted Grandpa.

"Come in! We're just sitting down to eat," called out one of Dan's aunts. Which one, he couldn't tell.

As the crowd filtered back into the kitchen, the center of all of the attention came into view.

At the site, Dan's eyes began to water.

Chapter 10

D AN'S DAD WALKED INTO THE room, receiving joyful relatives, kissing and hugging them. His dad stood smiling and chatting with each one as they approached him.

He appeared as he had in his mid-thirties, dressed in a short sleeved, cotton summer shirt with small alternating brown and tan squares. His blue jeans were clean and his black shoes polished to a bright shine. His hair was close cut and his face clean shaven. Everything about him exuded GI, a professional soldier.

Big tears came to Dan's eyes, and his heart ached at the site.

"Dad!" he burst out. His cry went unheeded.

He hadn't seen his dad for over twenty years when he had attended his funeral. That had been a struggle. His father had been neatly dressed, his dress blues and laid in an open casket for the viewing. Later, he would be dressed in his white temple clothes for the funeral itself. He had looked stately, as if he were merely sleeping.

Friends and relatives from all over had come to pay their respects and the room had been a bustle with reminiscence, as well as heartfelt tears. It wasn't until the next day that Dan realized how many people a life touches in its trek through life.

His dad had always been a quiet man, and you wouldn't have thought him so widely known. But he was a man who liked to help people and would often be found repairing someone's car or some kid's bicycle that happened to break down in front of the house. He had been very active in the Boy Scouts and had helped a great many a boy attain their Eagle Scout rank.

He remembered that on the day of the funeral the church was filled to bursting with relatives, neighbors, and Boy Scouts dressed in full uniform.

There had been a police escort to accompany the procession to the cemetery. It was long, and parking at the cemetery was at a premium. When the attendees were assembled at the graveside, the sound of *'Taps'* drifted on the breeze. This was followed by the sharp volley of a twenty-one gun salute. As the nation's flag was placed in his mother's lap, Dan remembered the feelings of longing, mixed with pride, which had filled his heart.

"Hoorah for the gospel," Dan whispered.

Reluctantly, the remembrance passed back into the recesses of his memory. Presently, he returned his focus to the here and now. His dad was ushered to a seat and given a plate on which to load food.

What he wouldn't give to have his mother see this. She had been alone these many years and had made the adjustment to living a single life. She was a tough lady, but he knew that she still missed him.

The sound of happy voices from the porch again caught his attention. "Mom?" he gasped. The very person he had been wishing was here walked in, hugging and laughing with the happy crowd of relatives. She, like Dad, was younger and more as he had remembered from his youth, her familiar grin lighting her face. She made her way into the kitchen and through to the living room.

The feast seemed to get into high gear with the arrival of Dan's parents. All involved ate to their hearts' content and reveled in their company. Dan found a corner of the living room where he sat down and watched as they mingled for what seemed a couple of hours.

He thought about Tammy, their kids, and the temple marriage that was so important to them. How he wished they were there with him to see. The crustiness and cynicism that had built up over the years seemed to be melting away. He felt a tenderness of heart that he hadn't felt in a long time. It was hard to fathom. He just couldn't feel cynical, and what a good feeling that was.

After a time, the family all gathered in the living room. They sat down and began to swap stories. Dan watched and listened from the corner. A story about a great uncle's car and the winter snows caught his interest. It seems that the uncle had stored an old jalopy in the lean-to shed that had once stood out behind the house. Two of the aunts recounted how they had played in the old car during the cold eastern Idaho winters of their youth. It was good fun for the two—then young girls—to climb into the old car and pretend they were travelling the world.

As the winter winds had begun to blow, the snows had swirled in, drifting around the machine as it sat silent in the shed, encasing it in a giant cocoon of white. When the snow had covered the old car from the top of the shed to the ground, the aunts had climbed onto the roof and slid merrily down, giggling as they went. It was all great fun until Grandma had discovered their activity and summarily put a stop to it. However, years later, they still chuckled as they remembered their clever exploits.

The guests laughed and joked with each other. There was a sereneness that seemed to fill the air. Dan watched from his corner afraid to move, afraid that it all would vanish if he disturbed the very air.

By now, the fear and tenseness he had experienced at the outset of the events were now things of the past. This unusual procession of spirits and phantoms had become surprisingly normal. And even though he was still afraid to disturb the air, the crowd of familiar spirits about him had strangely become comforting to him. He watched as his father laughed and chided his aunts. Dan's grandpa sat on the couch joking with one of the uncles, while Grandma sat quietly, a soft smile on her face as she watched the proceedings. It was then that everything got quiet.

Without warning, the apparitions sat down on the couch and chairs that seemed to form out of the air around them. As they sat, they turned their chairs in the same direction.

It was then that Dan realized they were all facing his corner of the room.

They were facing him.

Panic swelled in his breast. He now understood the phrase, "Cornered like a rat."

Were they aware of him? Did they see him? *Impossible!* he replied to the voice in his mind. *This is all a dream. I'll wake up anytime now. This isn't real.*

As if to add to his sudden panic, someone was calling his name. He looked around to see his dad standing in front of him, his hand extended, gesturing for him to join the family.

"This isn't real," he said out loud to himself, closing his eyes in an effort to make sense of it all. "This is PTSD coming home to roost," he chided himself, his eyes still closed.

He took a deep breath and tried to clear his head.

Chapter 11

"DAN...? SON...?" CALLED THE FAMILIAR voice.
"It's all in my head. It's got to be!" he told himself.

"No son, it's real," the voice assured him.

Dan slowly opened his eyes. The voice was that of his father, long since deceased. There he stood looking down at him, a concerned smile on his face. Dan nervously looked around; everyone was still there, watching him.

He slowly stood up and peered into the eyes of his father. "Who are you?" he asked guardedly.

"I am who you see that I am," came the reply.

His dad gestured for him to come and sit in a chair that had appeared. Dan hesitantly moved toward the chair. As he did so, he seemed to pass through some kind

of barrier that shimmered and stretched as he passed. It
clung to his body like a spider web, stretching, pulling,
until it finally gave way, allowing him to pass through.

As he sat down in the chair, the group of relatives
moved their own chairs into a semi-circle with Dan at the
center. His father pulled up a chair next to him.

The crowd of familiar faces sat silently as if waiting
for a signal or something from Dan. He noticed that the
apparitions, as he had seen them, were no longer mere
images of people he knew, but seemed to be solid living
beings. Where once they had appeared to be ciphers or
projections on the walls, they had made a complete
metamorphosis into solid three dimensional beings. No
longer did they pass by him without even a sideward
glance. They now were looking directly at him, aware of
his presence and him very much aware of theirs.

For a moment he sat in silence, taking it all in. "What
is this all about?" he asked, finally breaking the silence.

"It's a gift son," replied his father. "You see, you are
very special, and you have been chosen to carry on a
heritage, a history—*our* history. Do you remember how
many times you wondered what the walls would say if
only they could talk? Do you remember those times that
you looked at an old picture and wondered who those
people were, or what was the occasion? Your coming
here tonight was not a coincidence. It wasn't a chance
encounter that let you know that the house was to be

demolished. It wasn't by chance that you were able to get permission to visit from the contractor. No. These events were foreseen and put in motion long before you went to Oklahoma for training."

"That's right Danny," Grandpa spoke up. "We're here to seek your help. There are a great many things that have yet to happen. There are many people that need your help. Look around you." Grandpa swept his hand around toward the crowd of people in the living room. "I know you know most of us here, but look closer."

Dan glanced around the room. As he did so, people began to materialize. As more and more crowded into the room, it seemed to expand to accommodate them. Soon, there was a crowd of people that seemed to extend to the far reaches of what seemed eternity.

They were dressed in clothes from all the eras of time. There were men and women of every kind from all walks of life; some wore clothes of pioneers, others the garb of early 17th century businessmen. There were women with modest dresses and bonnets and others with clothes from the 1950's. There were soldiers, sailors, and airman from World Wars I and II, Korea, and Viet Nam. There were men from The Revolutionary and Civil Wars. Dan could see small children dressed in tattered pioneer clothes and other people dressed in the trappings of Rome.

People from all the eras of time stood silently waiting. Dan had risen from his chair and was standing, gazing, stunned, at the now full room.

"What is it I am to do?" he asked, his voice barely above a whisper.

Dan's father turned to him and said, "Seek them out. Find them. Help them. You have to do what I didn't know to do. These before you are all your family. They are your ancestors. I wish I had known to do more when I was in the world. But I learned too late and could only do a little before my mortal time was through. I'm doing what I can now do in the realm of spirits, but you know as I do that they cannot receive a fullness of joy without their ordinances. That is where you come in."

Dan felt a tear fill his eye. His heart began to swell as he looked at the longing faces. As silent as they remained, their eyes spoke volumes. A warm determination began to come over him. In his mind, the purposes of the temple had finally become clear. A new understanding of the 'why' etched itself in his consciousness. He felt the power of the Spirit coursing through his limbs, and that filled him with an indescribable joy.

As he stood watching the room began to fill with light, the personages before him were transformed. Their clothes changed becoming bright white robes, and their countenances shone with a heavenly glow. He noticed that people like his mother had disappeared, and only those who were deceased remained.

He turned again to his father. His dad smiled. "Dan, you have some time left here in this existence, but it will not be forever. Before you know it, you'll be here with us, and no more labor can be performed for those you see. Use your time wisely. Seek them. Find them. Help them. You'll do alright. Remember, we'll be waiting. I love you, son."

As his father finished speaking, the room again filled with the strange light which surrounded and engulfed each figure. Almost imperceptibly the light scattered as dust on a gentle breeze. The personages were gone and Dan found himself alone in the living room.

As he watched, the furniture and the trappings began to slide up the walls and become two dimensional as before. The colors faded and the walls once again appeared as a big black and white television screen.

The images seemed to gather in on themselves until they became a pinpoint of light that, without warning, blinked brightly, and then was gone leaving Dan standing in the empty room.

Presently, as his eyes adjusted to the darkness, he made his way back to the kitchen and the soft glow of the lantern. Dan stood in reverent silence, trying to wrap his mind around the whole night.

Slowly, and ever so quietly a warm confidence and assurance filled his heart. It had happened, and he knew it had. In the silence, he let the tears stream down his face.

Standing in the faint light of the kitchen, he bowed his head and uttered a heartfelt prayer of thanks.

He knew that he had been changed and would never be the same again.

Chapter 12

SLOWLY, THOUGHTFULLY, DAN GATHERED UP his gear and the old rotary telephone. For a moment, he stood taking it all in, one last time, and then walked out into the waning hours of the night.

As he bid farewell to the old house and its many memories, he felt lifted above the reach of the world.

The car rolled down the long driveway, and the crunch of the remaining gravel whispered his father's final admonition. *"Seek them out. Find them. Help them."*

Into the morning he drove with a renewed love for family, ancestors, and things eternal.

Create a Buzz!

Did you enjoy

Bakelite, a Rotary Dial, and a Party Line?

Please help spread the word.

Go to this link

http://weaverdm.weebly.com/buzz.html

for ways you can help.

Thanks!

♦ ♦ ♦

Coming Soon!

If you enjoyed D. M. Weaver's first novella,
you'll love his next!

Coming summer of 2015, his next book,
Winter's Light!

Sign up here

http://weaverdm.weebly.com/coming-soon.html

for pre-launch specials and notifications about each new
book and to continue following author D. M. Weaver as
they become available.

♦ ♦ ♦

About the Author

D. M. WEAVER WAS BORN IN Washington State into a military family. His childhood years were spent moving often with his family to different military bases around the globe.

He loved his childhood and grew to appreciate the unique experiences that are had by a boy growing up on the different army bases and small communities throughout the United States and the world. Not only does he enjoy military history, but his upbringing has made him keenly aware of the sacrifices made by those who have served their country.

His family background naturally steered him towards the life of a soldier, but as a young man, he sought to serve in a different kind of army. He decided to serve an LDS mission and spent two years in New Zealand. It was there that he learned to serve his Heavenly Father and His Son, Jesus Christ, as a missionary. He learned to love the Kiwis and the Polynesian people in all their variety. He made lifelong friends and took home an appreciation for people of different cultures. His dream is to one day visit the South Pacific again with his wife and someday serve another mission.

After his mission, Weaver embraced university studies at BYU–Provo. He graduated with his Bachelor of Science Degree in 1985.

He and his wife are presently raising their family in eastern Idaho where he works for the state and serves the Lord in whatever capacity he is called.

Weaver has always written poetry, jotting down thoughts and inspirations, and even short stories. At his wife's urging, he is now sharing that work. She is very proud of him, as are his children.

After going through a heart attack and quadruple bypass surgery, he says he has learned to lighten up and not take himself so seriously. He is learning to laugh more and enjoy life, for it can all change in a split second.

You can follow D. M. Weaver at:

http://weaverdm.weebly.com

♦ ♦ ♦